Our Emotions and Behavior

But Why Can't I?

Sue Graves

Illustrated by Desideria Guicciardini

free spirit
PUBLISHING®

Jenny came to look after Noah and his sister, Rosie. Mom told them the rules.

They had to go to bed at **7 o'clock.**
They had to listen to Jenny. They had
to follow the **rules.**

But Noah said rules **were silly!**

Jenny took them to the park.
They had to cross a road.

Jenny said there were **rules** for crossing roads.
They had to **stop**, **look**, and **listen**.

But Noah didn't **stop, look, or listen.**
He nearly ran into **the road!**

4

Jenny said **rules** can keep people safe!

Later on, Jenny got out a **game**.
She told them the **rules**.
They had to take turns rolling the dice.

6

But Noah didn't listen.
He didn't take turns.
No one could play.

So Jenny had to put the **game** away.

She said rules make *playing* games *fair!*

Then Jenny said it was **7 o'clock**.
It was time for bed.
But Noah didn't want to go to bed.
He wanted to stay up **late**.

"But why can't I?" he moaned.

Jenny said he needed his sleep.

She said people need sleep to keep **fit** and **healthy**.

11

But Noah didn't listen.
He stayed up **late**. He got
tired and **grumpy.**

12

13

Then Jenny told him that she had to follow **rules**, too.

She told him she worked in a store.
The store had lots of customers.
It was a great place to work.

But she had to follow the **rules**.
She had to look nice for work.

She had to get to work **on time**, too.

But one day Jenny was **late** for work.
The customers could not get into the store.
Everyone was angry.

Jenny nearly lost her job.
She was **never late again!**

Noah was really tired now.
He yawned and yawned.

Noah got under the blanket.
He said rules weren't silly at all!

Can you tell the story of Emma dropping her drink can on the path?

How do you think the boy who tripped felt?

Why do you think Emma should use the recycling bin?

A note about sharing this book

The **Our Emotions and Behavior** series has been developed to provide a starting point for further discussion about children's feelings and behavior, in relation both to themselves and to other people.

But Why Can't I?
This story explores in a reassuring way why we have rules and how rules can make everyone's lives easier and safer.

The book aims to encourage children to have a developing awareness of behavioral expectations in different settings. It also invites children to begin to consider the consequences of their words and actions for themselves and others.

Picture story
The picture story on pages 22 and 23 provides an opportunity for speaking and listening. Children are encouraged to tell the story illustrated in the panels: Emma drops her drink can on the path rather than using the recycling bin. A boy skates up and trips over the can. He is upset and Emma feels bad. She learns that using the bin might be a good rule after all.

How to use the book
The book is designed for adults to share with either an individual child or a group of children, and as a starting point for discussion.

The book also provides visual support and repeated words and phrases to build confidence in children who are starting to read on their own.

Before reading the story
Choose a time to read when you and the children are relaxed and have time to share the story.

Spend time looking at the illustrations and talking about what the book may be about before reading it together.

After reading, talk about the book with the children

- What was it about? Have the children ever had a babysitter? Did Mom or Dad lay down some rules? What were they? Did the children stick to the rules? If not, what were the consequences?

  Encourage the children to talk about their experiences.

- Extend this discussion by talking about other rules they know. Examples might be rules at home, rules in school, and rules when visiting other people's homes. Invite the children to talk about these rules and identify why they are important.

- Now talk about rules that apply to adults. Some examples might be parking restrictions, road rules, etc. Why do they think these rules are important? Conversely, can they think of any rules that they consider silly? Discuss the pros and cons of these rules.

- Take the opportunity to talk about rules that the children would like to see imposed to make their own lives easier. Examples might be stopping parents from parking too close to the school gates when dropping off and picking up their children.

- Look at the picture story. Ask the children to talk about Emma dropping her drink can on the path. Discuss why it would have been better for Emma to use the recycling bin.

  Can they think of other rules that help keep us safe in the park?

- Choose two settings, such as school and the playground, or the supermarket and the swimming pool. Make a list of rules for each setting and draw picture signs to decorate your rules lists. Compare the two lists. Are some rules the same? Are there any differences? Why?

Library of Congress Cataloging-in-Publication Data
Graves, Sue, 1950–
    But why can't I? / written by Sue Graves ; illustrated by Desideria Guicciardini.
        p. cm. — (Our emotions and behavior)
    ISBN 978-1-57542-376-0
    1. Children—Conduct of life—Juvenile literature. 2. Etiquette—Juvenile literature. 3. Social norms—Juvenile
literature. I. Guicciardini, Desideria. II. Title.
    BJ1631.G73 2011
    152.4—dc22
                                                                            2011001563
ISBN: 978-1-57542-376-0

Reading Level Grade 1; Interest Level Ages 4–8; Fountas & Pinnell Guided Reading Level I

10 9 8 7 6 5 4 3
Printed in China
S14100616

Free Spirit Publishing Inc.
6325 Sandburg Road, Suite 100
Minneapolis, MN 55427-3674
(612) 338-2068
help4kids@freespirit.com
www.freespirit.com

First published in 2011 by Franklin Watts, a division of Hachette Children's Books • London, UK, and Sydney, Australia

Text © Franklin Watts 2011
Illustrations © Desideria Guicciardini 2011

The rights of Sue Graves to be identified as the author and Desideria Guicciardini as the illustrator of this Work have
been asserted in accordance with the Copyright, Designs and Patents Act, 1988.

Editors: Adrian Cole and Jackie Hamley
Designers: Jonathan Hair and Peter Scoulding